NEW CREATION
One Man's Six Day Transformation

OLIVE SWAN

LIBERTY
UNIVERSITY
BOOKS

New Creation
by Olive Swan
© Copyright 2010. All rights reserved.

All rights reserved. No portion of this book may be reproduced by any means, electronic or mechanical, including photocopying, recording, or by any information storage retrieval system, without permission of the copyright's owner, except for the inclusion of brief quotations for a review.

ISBN-13: 978-1-935986-01-0

Cover & Interior Design:

Megan Johnson
Johnson2Design
Johnson2Design.com

A Division of Liberty University Press
Lynchburg, VA

*"Therefore, if anyone is in Christ, he is a new creation;
old things have passed away;
behold, all things have become new."*

II Corinthians 5:17

TABLE OF CONTENTS

Prologue 1
Genesis 1:1-2

Chapter One 9
Genesis 1: 3-5

Chapter Two 31
Genesis 1:7

Chapter Three 45
Genesis 1:9, 11a

Chapter Four 57
Genesis 1:14a

Chapter Five 65
Genesis 1:20

Chapter Six 77
Genesis 1:24, 26a, 27

Chapter Seven 85
Genesis 2:2

Chapter Eight 89
Genesis 2:18, 22-23

PROLOGUE

Genesis 1:1-2 "In the Beginning, God created the Heaven and the Earth. And the earth was without form and void and darkness was on the face of the deep."

The story broke on a Tuesday in September. It was the year of the greatest financial recession since the Great Depression. Banks and insurance companies, once thought untouchable, went belly up or were bought out by others. AIG, Fannie Mae and Freddie Mac, Merrill Lynch—they were all victims in one way or another. But while the eyes of the United States and the world were turned to Wall Street, the eyes of Chicago were averted to their own backyard.

Gregory Van Heeder was arrested by the Federal Bureau of Investigation at 8:13 a.m. today at the Chicago headquarters of United City Bank. Gregory, a vice president of the bank, is suspected of embezzling $3.2 million from his company.

NEW CREATION

Sean Wallace, a reporter for the *Daily Gazette*, paused to re-read the first paragraph, hoping he'd followed the inverted pyramid structure that newspaper articles were meant to follow. He knew his job was to write first, rewrite afterward, and his fingers sped over the keys as he added to the story.

This was big. Sean hoped it would be big enough to propel him from his job as reporter at the *Daily Gazette* in Arlington Heights to "the big time." He had passed the age of 25 just a few years previously, and before he hit his third decade of life, he wanted to be more than a beat reporter for a suburban newspaper. Single and living in a tiny apartment, his life revolved work and reaching his lofty goal. He wanted to be the next Pinch Sulzberger, publisher of the *New York Times,* or one of the lauded journalists with bylines in *USA Today*. Not that he didn't like the *Daily Gazette,* but it wasn't the *Chicago Tribune*. Or even the *Sun-Times* for that matter. But Sean attacked each story with a vigor he hoped would one day pay off for him. It didn't matter who he had to roll over in his quest for glory. He was all about number one.

"Sean."

He whipped his head up when he heard his boss, Vance Ibsen, call his name.

"Yes?"

"Come back to my office."

Sean followed obediently. He greeted Jeff Foutz, who was on the paper's public relations team.

PROLOGUE

"Sean, Jeff came to me with a great opportunity for you."

"Oh?" Sean asked, looking at Jeff with interest.

"I have an old friend, Bill Reeger," Jeff spoke up, "who is working for United City Bank in their public relations department."

Sean's brown eyes flared with animation and interest. "And?"

"Gregory Van Heeder's lawyer suggested they get a columnist to spend time with his daughter, write up positive human interest stories to generate goodwill for the family."

Sean paused. Putting up with a snobby elitist was not his idea of a good time, but it would allow him access to information no one else was getting.

"Does that mean I'd get leads that the other papers aren't?" he asked.

Jeff nodded. "Yep. This a great opportunity for the paper to learn things before our competitors."

Vance chuckled. "Bill Reeger must have owed you."

Jeff nodded. "Big time. So, Sean, will you take it?"

"I most certainly will." Sean answered right away. This may be a Pulitzer-winning story. There was a good chance his life wouldn't be the same after this.

With a knowing smile, Jeff handed Sean a slip of paper with an address.

"Here's the Van Heeder address. They have a gate, so let me call Bill and see if he can get the gate code from the lawyer."

Sean's blood was pumping. "Thanks."

NEW CREATION

"You'd better get going," Vance suggested. "We'll call when we get the code."

Sean took off without another word. With a quick stop at his desk to get his laptop, he headed down to his car. The rain that had apparently been trying to wash Chicago off the map had taken a break. Sean couldn't remember a more rainy September, and as he drove under the overcast sky, he couldn't help noticing how much the weather was like the news. Things were gray and cheerless in the headlines just as they were in the heavens.

He put on his blinker to get into the left turn lane as his phone buzzed at the incoming text. He read it and memorized the five-number gate code.

The drive from Arlington Heights to Kenilworth, where the Van Heeders had a lake estate, took a little over 30 minutes. Sean knew he had probably sped a bit, but didn't care. What were laws, if not meant to be broken?

Driving up to the Van Heeder estate, Sean had to make his way through press vans and reporters milling the street. Sean felt euphoria flood through his veins at his good luck. If he believed that there was a god, this would be one of the times when he would have said God was looking out for him. But Sean was agnostic, borderline atheist, and so he chalked up his good fortune to just that—fortune. Chance. As he punched in the numbers to the gate, letting it swing open, he couldn't help feeling that it was his lucky day.

Sean parked behind a white Lexus with gold detailing and stepped out of his car. He made his way to the double oak front

PROLOGUE

doors, noting the immaculate landscaping and the view of the lake, which was running over from the rains. Had the Van Heeder home not been so well placed on a rise in the land, it would have been in danger of flooding, but as it was, there seemed to be no worries for the Van Heeders in that respect. Sean noticed all this in an instant as he made his way up to the door.

Sean knocked and waited. After a few moments, a woman answered the door. Her eyes were red-rimmed and her cheeks were pink. She'd been crying. She was in her late 50s, Sean guessed, and resembled the picture of Gregory Van Heeder that Sean had looked up on the United City Bank website. She was probably a sister to Gregory. She carried herself with a bearing that was unmistakably well-bred. Despite the watery eyes that she studied him with, not a hair was out of place, not one wrong crease, stain, or tear upon her clothes. Sean was impressed by the deep sense that this woman was not pleased to see him at all.

"Yes?" she asked.

"Bill Reeger told me you were expecting me."

"Oh, the reporter," she intoned.

Sean heard the bite in her words and denied himself the sneer that wanted to spring to his lips. Reporters might not be the best-loved people in the world, but he wasn't the one sitting at the jail.

"Yes, I'm Sean Wallace."

She stepped back and reluctantly murmured, "Come in," leading him to the living room. Sean ignored the surroundings as he took in a young woman sitting on the sofa.

NEW CREATION

Esmerelda Delaney Van Heeder. Gregory's daughter.

Sean had researched the family before coming and knew that Esmerelda was recently out of college and a few years younger than he was. She was beautiful, no doubt about that. She had blond hair—the kind of Nordic blond that people expect of the Dutch and upper Scandinavians. She was above average for a woman—seven or eight inches over five feet. If she wore heels, she'd be Sean's own six-foot height.

Esmerelda looked as if she'd been crying as well. There was a sheen of tears in her eyes as she looked at the man sitting on the sofa next to her talking in a quiet voice. Sean noted the jeans and the college sweatshirt and the messy ponytail into which she'd pulled her long locks. When they noticed their guest, they stopped talking and looked up at him.

"Essie, Jarrod, this is Sean," the hostess said quietly.

Sean stepped forward to shake hands. Jarrod's grip was firm, and Esmerelda's was too, for a fragile-looking young woman. There was a different confidence in the young woman's welcome than that of the older woman who had opened the door. It did not come from an extrinsic placement of price and position, but in intrinsic value of calmness and serenity.

"I'm Jarrod Perry from Blackwell and Ellis law firm," the man said. "This is my wife, Nancy, and this is Gregory's daughter and my niece, Esmerelda."

"Hello, Mr. Perry. Ms. Van Heeder."

Jarrod took Sean's arm and led him aside so that Esmerelda and Nancy couldn't hear what the men were talking about.

PROLOGUE

"I told Mr. Reeger that I wanted a good journalist to help with the PR on this story," Jarrod informed Sean.

"Of course."

"I want someone who will treat this with sensitivity and objectivity."

Sean nodded with fake sincerity. "Obviously objectivity is the key," he replied. *Unless it doesn't sell,* he thought to himself. He sat down as Esmerelda and Jarrod discussed the timeline of the case. He jotted down notes on when the arraignment was to be held and any other court appearances.

"Will you be freezing our assets?" Esmerelda asked her uncle.

"I'm going to find that out tomorrow, Essie. I'll let you know after the press conference."

Esmerelda nodded. "Yes, find out and let me know. Until then, do I have control of my father's money?"

Jarrod nodded. "Yes, you do."

"What are you going to do with it?" Nancy asked.

"I don't know, Aunt Nancy." Esmerelda dropped her head into her hands and took an audible shuddering breath. "I just don't know," she finished in a whisper.

Aunt Nancy stood, took Esmerelda's arm and helped her up.

"Come on, Dear. Let's get you upstairs. It has been a long day."

Sean watched them ascend the staircase. He turned to Jarrod.

"Tomorrow we have a press conference at the bank," Jarrod said. "We're meeting here at 7 a.m."

NEW CREATION

Sean nodded. "I'll be here."

He left the estate, passing the stringers, reporters, cameramen, and radio newsmen that were wrapping up cords and loading the news vans. He needed to get home; he had a column to write. *New York*, he grinned, *Here I come.*

CHAPTER ONE

Genesis 1:3-5 "Then God said, "Let there be light"; and there was light. And God saw the light, that it was good; and God divided the light from the darkness. God called the light day, and the darkness He called night. So the evening and the morning were the first day."

There was a posse of reporters around the Van Heeder estate the next morning when Sean pulled into the driveway. He parked in the grass behind the same white Lexus. The garage door was open and there were two more upscale cars inside. Sean's Toyota Prius contrasted sharply with the luxury vehicles. He got out and walked inside.

Jarrod Perry was sitting at the dining room table looking through papers. He looked up when Sean entered and shuffled the papers back together and zipped them into a brown leather portfolio.

NEW CREATION

Sean moved to the window and noticed a chauffeur backing the Mercedes out of the garage. They heard footsteps on the stairs and Sean turned around and saw Esmerelda coming down the steps ahead of her aunt. Unlike the casual outfit from the day before, she had certainly dressed to impress today. She was wearing a conservative gray suit with a pencil skirt that fell to her knees. Underneath the tailored jacket was a blouse with a muted pattern. Her hair had been pulled back and pinned up. Her makeup was light and understated.

Sean couldn't help admiring her. He wondered if he could turn on the Wallace charm, show a little bit of caring, write a good column about her. Maybe pretend to be her friend in her time of trial. Sean smiled slyly on the inside. This could be a great assignment. His goal was clear, be the inside guy for the story, use it as leverage for a better job, and add Essie Van Heeder to his list of conquests. Broken-hearted women needed someone to turn to, and could usually be persuaded to be amorous. With her father in jail, Sean was guessing that Esmerelda needed love. But he didn't let any of his thoughts show on his face as he followed the Perrys and Esmerelda outside.

They headed out to the cars. Sean angled himself so that as Esmerelda reached the Mercedes, he had already waved the chauffeur away and gallantly opened the back door for her. She finally looked into his eyes.

"Thank you," she murmured politely, in a perfectly developed tone of silky smoothness.

He let her in and then quickly slid in next to her. "Hope you don't mind my riding with you."

CHAPTER ONE

"Very well."

Sean knew she was too well-bred to refuse. Jarrod and Nancy were taking their own car. Sean knew he could have driven himself, but he needed to ask Esmerelda some questions.

He pulled out his notepad. "So, how would you describe your father?"

He could almost guess the words Essie would use. "Caring, thoughtful, intelligent, under-appreciated." People whose family had committed such crimes usually tried to make the criminal sound not so bad.

Essie kept her gaze looking out the window. "He's no better or worse than anyone else."

Sean furrowed his eyebrows. That seemed like a strange thing to say. "I don't quite understand."

"We're all sinners. He's no different."

"Sinners?" Sean saw a red light flashing in his brain. The term brought back Sundays at St. Agnes's Catholic Church his family attended.

She turned to look at him and smiled dryly. "Yes. No one is perfect before God."

God. There was that word. Sean tucked this knowledge away. He'd grown up Catholic, but for the last 10 years he hadn't given God a thought. He had moved out of his parent's home at 18, hating the unbending loyalty his parents gave their church. On the other hand, adding religion to the story would cause the Christians to feel bad for her. Those with logical, rational brains

NEW CREATION

would see how useless religion was; it hadn't kept Mr. Van Heeder from embezzling money. Yes, Sean was determined. He would add the fact about her Christianity. It would play both sides perfectly. People certainly saw what he wanted them to, didn't they?

"Maybe not," he finally answered Essie. "But if he is indeed guilty, he's stolen money from the poor that is not his. How would you justify that?"

"You don't," Essie admitted.

Her eyes narrowed as they pierced his own. Sean had the vague feeling that she could see through him. To turn the awkward feeling away, he poked deeper into her hurt and pain.

"I don't think the average reader would appreciate that your father doesn't care about the common worker or person on the street," he said, unable to keep the bite out of his words.

"You will focus on the common man or the poor person as long as it will keep you from looking at yourself, where the same evil that brought my father to this rests in your own heart, won't you?"

And with those words, Essie turned back to look out the window. Sean sat back, floored by her words. He hadn't met many people who could string such condemning words together so quickly. Typical Christian. Always blaming someone else.

They reached United City Bank's headquarters and a bank PR man met them. He held the door for Essie and helped her out.

"Hello, Miss Van Heeder."

"Hello, Max. How are you?"

CHAPTER ONE

"I'm okay. And you?"

"I've been better," she replied with a weak smile. "But tell me, is Mr. Arbondnut, the bank president, going to see me privately before the press conference?"

"Yes, he told me to convey you to his office as soon as you were here."

"Lead away," she smiled graciously.

She followed Max into the building with her entourage following along behind. The news photographers waiting at the entrance were snapping photos, filling the air with lights and lenses. Sean noticed a photographer from the *Daily Gazette*. He gave the man a wave and headed in behind Jarrod and Nancy. The small group was taken up to a top floor where the executive offices were located, offices that Esmerelda had frequented with dignity until recently. Now Sean knew she could only enter them with discomfort.

Sean took out his digital camera and hung back as the party made their way to the bank president's waiting room. Sean wanted pictures of Van Heeder's office. There was a gray pallor to the room from the overcast sky outside that seemed fitting for the effect he wanted. The Feds had carried out all the files and the room was practically empty—open file drawers, a desk with no computer. He snapped several photos and then hurried to the waiting room. Tbe Perrys were waiting with Max. Sean went over to the administrative assistant.

"Would you like to give me your impressions of yesterday morning?"

NEW CREATION

The woman, like all people who have witnessed law enforcement officials in action, was eager to talk. Sean recorded her on tape but also scribbled in shorthand the details she gave him. She had a good memory. With his imagination, Sean was able to see it all. He replayed what it must have looked like to see the FBI agents entering the building just after 8 a.m. They would have made their way to the top floor and asked to see Gregory. There, in his office, they would have arrested him and led him down in handcuffs. Sean tried to visualize the reactions of the workers. As Gregory was escorted down with his head bowed in shame, Mr. Arbondnut watched from his office door, his face a mask of disappointment. The employees gathered around in shock.

"Thank you so much, Mrs. Agman. Tell me, would you have expected Mr. Van Heeder to do this?" he inquired quietly, not wanting to disturb Nancy and Jarrod across the room.

"No, it was a huge surprise. He's always been a friendly man. He's never mentioned if he had problems with the other executives. Very charismatic."

The best thieves always were, Sean thought. "Uh-huh. Tell me, what do you think about his daughter?"

Mrs. Agman frowned. "I feel very badly for Esmerelda. She comes to visit her dad quite a bit and always has nice things to say to everyone. There isn't anyone who dislikes her."

"Like father, like daughter?"

"Yeah, I guess you could say that. I've known her quite a long time. She's a lot like him. Quiet, but intelligent. He's a bit more talkative than she is."

CHAPTER ONE

"I see."

Mr. Arbondnut and Esmerelda exited the room. They both looked solemn. The gray-haired bank president spoke, his voice strong, but sorrowful. "Are you ready, Max? Mr. Reeger is waiting for us."

He headed down to the conference room. The rest of the group followed him. There were only a few reporters in the room, and Sean pulled out the questions he'd written. He didn't know if there were to be questions, but he was ready just in case.

Bill Reeger spoke first, assuring the press that the bank was still in a solid financial position and that they were taking the best steps to resolve the problem. He then introduced Esmerelda and she stepped up to the microphone.

"This is a horrible tragedy to befall the bank. If my father is guilty of this"—Sean knew that Jarrod wouldn't let her say that her father was guilty—"then I will do what I can to make it right."

Esmerelda was calm and stood without embarrassment or shame although Sean, and apparently the rest of the throng, expected it.

With that she stepped down and Mr. Arbondnut stepped up. With a mature gravity, he accepted Esmerelda's statement and reiterated Mr. Reeger's remarks. The press conference ended without questions.

Jarrod led Esmerelda out and as the room emptied, Sean was pushed to the back of the crowd. He had to hurry to catch up to Esmerelda and her relatives. They went down to the cars.

NEW CREATION

Bill got in the back of Jarrod's Lexus and Sean once again rode with Esmerelda.

"So exactly what does that mean, you'll do all you can to make things right?" he inquired of her.

"Well, I don't want to make it public yet, but I'm making restitution."

"Is that a Biblical idea?" Sean asked as they rode back to the Van Heeder home.

Esmerelda nodded. "Yes, it is. Do you know the Bible?"

"I grew up going to church."

"That doesn't mean you know the Bible."

Sean sighed. He gave his voice a pleading, tender quality. "What can I do to make you realize that I'm not your enemy, Miss Van Heeder? I'm here to help get public opinion on your side."

Esmerelda studied his face. His words were too conciliatory, his manner too slick. "I don't trust you," she admitted to him. "But if your approach to writing these columns is objective and honest, then I am more than willing to work with you."

"Naturally. I'm a blank slate. My mind is open. Tell me, what are you going to do to pay restitution?" He quietly flipped on his tape recorder.

"Sell the house. Or, let the bank take it over. Sell the cars. Liquidate the things in the house. Find new positions for the cook and chauffeur."

"Where will you live?"

CHAPTER ONE

"I have my own money. I'll find a job. Get an apartment," she spoke simply, easily, as if discussing the rainy weather and not the complete dismantling of her plush life.

"Would the Perrys take you in?"

Esmerelda shook her head. "I can't do that to them. Besides, it's time I stood on my own two feet."

"That's very brave of you. I'm sure people will pity you."

"I almost pity them."

"Why? Because they're poorer than you?"

She shook her head. "No, because it's easy to get wrapped up in the treasures of this world and forget that eternity is what matters. Losing everything is a hard way for me to be reminded, but I'll get through it. God has blessed me with many other things."

"That's true," Sean agreed, although he couldn't seem to follow her train of thought. Treasures, eternity, what?

"You probably don't understand what I'm saying," she responded patiently.

Sean shrugged. "You'll probably still have money left over even after you provide restitution to the people wronged. You know, I bank at United City Bank," he lied.

"Oh, would you like me to cut you a check now?" she quipped caustically as her eyes bore into his.

He got the strange sense she could read his thoughts and see through to the lies. For a man who kept his thoughts and emotions away from public view, he didn't like the feeling. He chuckled nervously, feeling as if he were caught.

NEW CREATION

"I'm kidding."

She gave him a knowing look. "Of course."

The conversation ended. Still, there was a bit of unease in Sean's spirit. It was as if he were one pointed question away from opening the curtain between the false substance he'd built in front of his soul to hide the void beyond.

They reached the Van Heeder home and Sean took his laptop from his car into the house and set it up to type the draft of his column. He kept his ear tuned to the conversations around him. He heard Aunt Nancy ask Esmerelda if she were going to church that night. Esmerelda said she was. Bill took his leave after a short session with Jarrod. Jarrod took his briefcase and portfolio and kissed his wife goodbye and left for his office.

"I'll see you tomorrow at the arraignment," he told Esmerelda, and was out the door.

Sean started typing away. His cell phone buzzed and he took the call outside.

"Hello, Sean here."

"Hi, Sean. It's Vance."

"Hello."

"What do you have?"

"Quite a bit. I got a great lead, but I can't break it yet. Maybe in one or two days. But stay posted."

"Great. Get as much as you can."

CHAPTER ONE

"Do you want me to keep doing this as hard news or more as human interest?"

"Hmm. Keep doing it hard news."

"Okay."

"Your last column was great. A lot more information than what the other papers had. Thank goodness Jeff knew Bill. Having you in there is awesome."

"Thanks."

"No, thank you, Sean. Talk to you later."

Sean closed his phone and entered the house. Nancy was sitting in the living room with a book as Esmerelda paced around with a phone to her ear. From her conversation, it sounded to Sean that she was trying to find the cook a job. Although he was usually hardened to the world and its ills, he realized that such a gesture was good of Esmerelda. Most people would just lay off the person with a "have a nice day." In this economic climate, finding a job was very difficult. To actually go through all that work to find the woman another employer was loving.

Sean's fingers paused over the keys. What was it that made one person steal $3.2 million from his employers when his net worth was probably more, yet his own daughter took time from her day to find a mere domestic servant a new position? Why was that? Probably Esmerelda was just young and hadn't lived very long in the business world. If she were her father's age, she would be tempted to do the exact same as Gregory, Sean thought bitterly. Still, deep down, he had a tiny bit of respect for her.

NEW CREATION

"What time are you going to church?" Nancy asked Esmerelda when her niece got off the phone.

"It starts at 6:30. I'll probably leave at 6."

"Did you want me to go with you?" Nancy asked.

"I'd like it if you would."

"It's just that everyone will look at us strangely," her aunt fussed.

"I'll take you," Sean spoke up.

Esmerelda looked up at him in surprise. "What?"

"Sure. Your aunt has had a long day."

Nancy actually gave him a smile.

"Oh, all right," Esmerelda replied.

Sean finished his article and e-mailed it to his copywriter and then closed his laptop.

"I've got some things to take care of at work."

"Can I read the article you wrote?" Esmerelda asked.

Sean looked down at his laptop. "Uh, that wasn't my article," he smiled, as the deception passed his lips.

She raised her eyebrow. "No?"

"Nope. But I'll have it for you when I come get you. You can read it then."

"All right," she softly replied.

Sean bid her goodbye and left the house feeling relieved. That was one astute woman. He strongly doubted that she'd be so eas-

CHAPTER ONE

ily duped into sleeping with him. He headed home and dumped his laptop down and headed out for a beer with his friend Tyson.

When he was slightly buzzed and mellow enough that he figured he could get through a night at a church, he headed home to brush his teeth, change, and pick up Esmerelda.

"My chauffeur will drive us," she informed him when he got there. You are still welcome to come, of course."

There was no reason for Sean to go with, except that his dreams for a better future hung on getting the most information out of her. He agreed to ride along. "Okay."

Sean was not surprised that the chauffeur was driving them. There was no way Esmerelda was going to be able to live any other way than in the lap of luxury. When they were seated on the comfortable leather seats, she glanced at him.

"I hope you're not insulted."

"Why?"

"Because I didn't think it was safe for me to ride alone with you."

Sean cleared his throat. "No, of course not. You did the right thing."

He looked out the window. Her admission hurt a bit. Naturally she wouldn't feel safe with him, and it was smart of her to have someone with her. He just didn't like his integrity questioned. Not that integrity was a respected word or character trait among him and his friends.

NEW CREATION

"I do apologize if I've hurt your feelings."

Her voice cut into his thoughts. He waved his hand.

"Don't apologize. You did the smart thing. You hardly know me. You have no reason to trust my integrity. I'm sure you'll get to realize I'm a good guy."

"You are?"

Sean smiled. "Of course."

"Did you bring the article?"

"I forgot."

"I understand. Well, I can read it in the newspaper."

"Do you like reading the newspaper?"

"Sometimes."

"Why 'sometimes'?"

"Because the obvious bias of journalists bothers me."

"Oh, really."

"Yes. There's a definite slant against Christianity … the words you use to put doubt into people's minds about us. We're not perfect, but oftentimes we're made out to look hypocritical. Yet Christianity is the basis of our nation."

"I've always thought that religion was a blight, a scar upon our nation." He started to get angry thinking about it. "People subscribing to a God that only takes certain people to heaven. Doesn't let us live how we want to. That's ridiculous."

She didn't hesitate to answer. "It is belief in God that gave us

CHAPTER ONE

the independence to yearn for freedom and have a work ethic to succeed. Would you not want us to have that?"

Sean thought about that. He loved politics but not many women would discuss it with him, even to disagree.

"Well, I think we should agree to disagree," he said breezily, finding it a struggle to think up a good argument.

"All right," she patiently murmured.

When they reached the church, the chauffeur parked and they walked up to the stone building.

"What's going on at church tonight?" Sean questioned.

"Prayer meeting."

"Are you going to ask for prayers for yourself?"

"No. I'm going to pray for you."

Sean watched as she headed into the sanctuary. He sat in the back row, not willing to get too involved.

There was a man standing at a wooden podium in front of the pulpit. He greeted them all with a smile.

"It's good to see everyone here. Do we have prayer requests?"

Sean remembered prayer requests at St. Agnes. Cancer, heart problems, diabetes—you name any medical condition, the people there probably had it. As people started giving their prayer requests, Sean noticed a marked difference this time, though. There were prayer requests for families that were "running away from God," sons and daughters at war, strength to witness, grace and mercy for co-workers. True, some mentioned medical problems

NEW CREATION

as well. But Sean was surprised at the outward focus the people had. They thought more of others and not of themselves. Finally Esmerelda slipped her hand up.

"Yes, uh, Esmerelda," the leader said.

Everyone turned in their seat to see her. Sean saw all the emotions on their faces: pity, kindness, anger, distrust, inquisitiveness.

"I'd like prayer for my father."

The leader nodded and jotted it down. "Of course."

After about five minutes of taking requests and hearing praises, of which there were many (to Sean's amazement), they split up into groups. Esmerelda was joined by two middle-aged women and the three sat in a small group at the back of the church near Sean's pew. He listened to their prayers.

When it got to Esmerelda's turn, her prayer was short, but full of passion and emotion. Sean had heard of people who prayed like God was in the room, but hadn't heard it for himself. As Esmerelda talked to God, Sean could almost see her standing before Him sharing her requests.

"God, you know about what my father did. Please help him to see his wrong as You do. Help me as I have to make so many changes in my life now. For Aunt Nancy and Uncle Jarrod. They don't know you except in a merely knowledgeable way. They don't yet have the peace that passes understanding that you give. Please bless them and show them that peace."

Although impressed with the sound of her sincere prayer, Sean listened and in silence mocked her in his heart.

CHAPTER ONE

She took a deep breath and continued. "And Lord, I pray for Sean. He's blinded to your truth and I just pray that you would send your Spirit to open his eyes."

Sean was floored, rancor leaving him in an instant. Esmerelda was praying for him! True, he didn't think it would mean anything, since he wasn't sure that there was a God. But if it helped her get through this time, then certainly that was her prerogative to pray to Him.

Sean suddenly wished he could know for sure that there was a God or not. Until now, he battled with the idea that you couldn't know for certain. He didn't realize until standing next to Esmerelda who lived as if God were alive, that he would rather know one way or the other.

"God, if you really are there, if you really exist, open my eyes," he prayed quietly.

Nothing miraculous happened and Sean shrugged. There must not be a God. Maybe now he could stop wondering about it. When the prayer was over, Esmerelda stood and talked quietly with the two women for a few minutes before they both gave her a hug and gathered their things.

"Ready to go?" Sean asked.

"Nope. I have children's club tonight."

"What?"

"Are you staying?"

"Well, you are my ride," he replied bitterly.

NEW CREATION

"Okay. Wait here."

She departed into the bathroom and returned about a minute later having changed into more casual clothes.

Sean sighed and followed her into the children's area. He stuck close by Esmerelda all night. She was a helper with the young age group, 3 and 4 years old, and Sean had never been around such small kids. He was the youngest of his family and he couldn't remember if he'd ever even held a child.

Sean watched with something close to awe as Esmerelda patiently helped the tiny children play their games. He could not believe how joyful Esmerelda's face looked as she laughed with them and clapped for them. When games were done, they gathered in small groups and Esmerelda sat at a table two feet off the ground in a chair several sizes too small to listen to the children recite a Bible passage with their high voices. Sean listened to them, amazed at their ability to memorize the verses. True, the verses weren't long, but he'd never done anything like that. He could memorize the Cubs' lineup and their yearly stats, but how important was that in the face of mounting economic struggles, natural disasters, and a controversial political scene?

"Good job, Maggie, you did that verse perfectly," Esmerelda congratulated a small, dark-haired girl.

The girl smiled brightly and threw her arms around Esmerelda, who gave her a loving hug back. Sean looked at his watch. Almost eight o'clock. In 14 hours, Esmerelda's father would stand before a judge at his arraignment. But none of that mattered to

CHAPTER ONE

Maggie who looked up at Esmerelda with adoration in her young, innocent eyes.

"It's time to go listen to the Bible story," Esmerelda said.

Sean followed them into the children's chapel and lowered himself Indian style onto the floor. He figured it would either be Moses and the bulrushes, Joseph of the wild coat, or Jesus in the manger—no wait, that was Christmastime. He was surprised when the teacher started out at the beginning of the Bible, in Genesis.

"God made everything!" the teacher said.

Sean wanted to scoff. What a crock. Everyone knew that the universe had been started at least 14 billion years ago from the big bang.

"Only God can create from nothing," the teacher was informing them.

Sean rolled his eyes. "Yeah right," he murmured under his breath.

"And God made it perfect. When he created it, there was no bad thing. Animals ate plants, and Adam and Eve didn't have any arguments. But then, you know what happened, Eve and Adam ate the fruit they weren't supposed to. As soon as they did, the earth was cursed. Lions started eating gazelles. Thorns grew. Their own son killed his brother. This wouldn't have happened if Adam had obeyed God."

Sean had never heard that before. How did the teacher know that? He figured Esmerelda would know. He'd ask her in the car on the way home.

NEW CREATION

Esmerelda was excited to share when Sean brought it up later. "Yes, the world was perfect until Adam sinned. That's why there's evil in the world. God is good and created good. He didn't create evil. Evil is the absence of good, just as dark is the absence of light, so when Adam sinned, he introduced evil into the world. That's why there is war, children dying of hunger, and even numerous other sins like lying."

"I can't say as I believe you."

"One day God will restore the world to good again."

"If there is a God. It seems like you have a false hope."

"And by your belief in a world created by time, chance, and death, you have no hope at all."

Sean couldn't answer.

"Tell you what, Sean. Since I've been forced to have you follow me around for your news columns, promise me you'll read some books."

"About what?"

"The fossil record, the universe, why evolution couldn't be true statistically."

"No one believes that God created it," he scoffed.

"Then why are evolutionists so insistent on it not even being discussed in schools?"

"Because it's so outlandish!"

"No more outlandish than random hydrogen atoms suddenly bursting into a universe that is so orderly it follows numerous natural laws," she stressed.

CHAPTER ONE

Sean was again speechless and hated the feeling. He would read those books just to see how ridiculous the whole idea was.

"I'll read the books. Get them for me."

At Esmerelda's house, he waited while she rustled around her library for the books. She came out with a stack. Sean took them, a little surprised at the volume of information on her position. How come he didn't know there were so many things written on creation? He thought it was just an old fable from the Bible that only deluded church-goers believed. But he'd promised he would read the books. Good thing he loved reading.

"Uh-thanks."

"Sure," she replied with a smile. "Are you coming to the arraignment tomorrow?"

"Yes."

"All right. Goodbye, Sean. Thanks for coming with me tonight."

"Sure. Uh, thanks for praying for me."

She smiled. "Of course."

She closed the door and Sean walked to his car. What an interesting few days. He drove home and parked and then carried the stack of books up to his apartment. He opened the first one and was soon lost in the pages. He'd never known that paleontologists had found marine creature fossils above fossils of creatures that supposedly had lived millions of years later, or that they'd found cancer in bones of a dinosaur. And the books on evolution's beginnings and logical conclusions were eye-opening. It

NEW CREATION

was a hopeless system of randomness. Never had he realized anything so clearly. It suddenly struck him that if it were true, then his desire to be an editor was merely the accidental arrangement of atoms. What, then, gave his reaching for the goal any purpose or necessity? He began to feel his strong belief in the survival of the fittest slipping, and he put the books away. He turned his light out and laid on his side trying to sleep. Without evolution, his whole philosophy of life was in danger of crumbling. He was beginning to see that there weren't just slight disagreements between him and Esmerelda. Their worldviews, beliefs, and lifestyles were as different as night and day.

CHAPTER TWO

Genesis 1:7 "Thus God made the firmament, and divided the waters which were under the firmament from the waters which were above the firmament; and it was so."

For the arraignment, Esmerelda dressed in black slacks with a sea green top that brought out the blue of her icy ocean eyes. She was not looking forward to the next few hours. Nervousness filled her as she realized this would be the first time she'd see her father since Tuesday morning, when he'd kissed her forehead goodbye before going to work.

She straightened her hair and pushed the strands behind her ear. For some reason she looked vulnerable when she saw her reflection in the mirror.

"Esmerelda!" she heard her Aunt Nancy call from downstairs.

She grabbed her purse and went to meet her aunt and uncle. When they

NEW CREATION

pulled up to the courthouse, Sean was waiting for them. He helped Esmerelda out of the car.

"Have you started the books?" she questioned.

"Yes. It's eye opening."

She smiled. "Good. Let's hope it's mind- and heart-opening as well."

Sean decided to ignore her insinuation that he was narrow-minded and gently took her elbow. They walked inside the courtroom, where Esmerelda slipped into the front row behind the defendant's table. Jarrod was sitting there looking over his papers. The door on Esmerelda's left opened and a policeman entered leading Gregory. He carried himself like a shamed man. His head was down and he shuffled into the room.

He looked up and his eyes met Esmerelda's. Sean looked at the young woman. Her hand had come to her throat and was gripping the buttons on her blouse near her neck.

Gregory's eyes turned anxious when he saw his daughter, but he didn't speak. He sank down into his chair and folded his hands in front of him.

The judge entered and they all rose. After the lawyers' arguments had been heard and the evidence looked at, the judge decreed the case worthy of trial. Esmerelda let out a long breath. Sean was sitting in the row behind the family and when he heard a sniff, he glanced at Aunt Nancy who was wiping tears from her eyes. Sean was taking down notes furiously at everything he was hearing. He couldn't help feeling euphoria at the awesome advantage to the story he had been given.

CHAPTER TWO

The judge set bail in the hundreds of thousands of dollars and Gregory was taken away.

"I have to talk to him," Esmerelda muttered.

Jarrod came over, defeated at the case going to trial.

"Will you go see him?" he asked Esmerelda.

Esmerelda nodded. "Yes."

"Do you have the money for his bail?"

Esmerelda shook her head. "No. No I don't."

Sean scribbled furiously. They made their way to the room where Van Heeder was being held.

"Dad!" Esmerelda called. Her voice broke as she ran to her father. She put her arms around his neck and started to weep.

"Oh, Essie, I'm so sorry," he said.

Nancy was crying, and Jarrod looked ready to break down as well. Essie held her father and cried on his shoulder.

"Dad, Dad, why?" she sobbed.

"I just wanted you to be happy," he replied, anger in his voice.

"I was!" she insisted. "What more did I need? I had a father who loved me, a home, a car, and a good name. It's all gone! You're being taken from me."

"No, I'm not, Essie. We'll fight this. Post bail and I can go home."

"No, Dad. I can't."

Gregory's mouth fell open. "What, what do you mean?" his voice broke. "Essie, what are you saying?"

NEW CREATION

She wiped the tears from her eyes. "You always taught me that actions had consequences. You have to live with the punishment of your actions."

"I did this for you," he cried, deluding himself but no one else in the room.

"No, Dad," she wept. "You did this for yourself. You just wanted more. You hurt people. You stole."

Gregory couldn't justify himself in the face of her stark condemnation, instead, he just cried. Sean watched this scene, noting the difference between Gregory and his daughter. Esmerelda was crying tears of sorrow that her father had broken the law. Gregory wept because of anger and bitterness. He was angry that he'd been caught, not that he'd done wrong.

Sean stopped writing, caught in a rare moment of personal analysis. How often had he truly been sorry for lying? For the girls whose hearts he'd broken? For the hatred toward people he may have disagreed with? He hurried on with his writing, hoping that the moment of self-reflection would pass quickly. Esmerelda hated the tears in her father's eyes, but knew she couldn't in good conscience bail him out of jail.

"No, Dad. I can't keep you from your punishment. You did wrong. Besides, a good part of the estate is going to pay back United City Bank for the money you stole."

"It wasn't stealing. It was just a numbers game."

"You took money you didn't earn. That's stealing."

Sean felt guilt bite him. He'd played that game, too — the "let's just change the terms so it's not so bad" game. Wasn't his po-

CHAPTER TWO

litical party interested in "redistribution?" That was taking money from some people and giving it to others through the income tax. Was that stealing? If Sean thought about it, the answer would be yes. He gulped.

The policeman cleared his throat. "Let's go, Van Heeder."

Esmerelda held onto her father until the policeman separated them. Nancy came over and the two women held each other and cried. Once again, Sean was struck by the difference in the tears. Nancy was obviously overwhelmed by hopelessness. Esmerelda was sorrowful. For her father, her family, and for the whole mess. Sean felt his admiration for her grow. It couldn't be easy to refuse to post bail, but she had her convictions. It may have seemed heartless, yet it was obvious the love she had for her father. Sean wondered if there was a man in her life that she loved as much as her dad. He shook his head to clear the desire to be that man. He didn't want to be tied down, and women like Esmerelda required fidelity—for a lifetime.

Gregory was taken away and Jarrod led his weeping wife and niece out. Sean followed, his heart divided. Part of him wanted to rush off and write the story, the other wanted to hide it away, keep the depth of emotion from the world's prying, insatiable eyes. He felt, as he walked away with his notepad in hand, that in that room someone had taken a magnifying glass to his heart. And he wanted to know what exactly they saw.

Back at the spacious Van Heeder home, Esmerelda nibbled away at the appetizers the cook had set in the living room. Her

35

NEW CREATION

eyes were red-rimmed, and at intervals she would stop and rub the tears away. When she was composed, she'd return to what she had been doing. Aunt Nancy was lying down in the guest room with a cold washcloth on her forehead.

Sean puttered around with his laptop, munching on the appetizers. In the last two days, he'd been with the family most of the day, but since this was his column, he hadn't needed to be at the office. He looked down at the document. He'd started writing it in a more soft-news, human interest tone. He grimaced. Where had the hard-nosed journalist gone?

"Are you okay?" he heard Esmerelda ask from across the table.

"Yes. I am. Are you?" he asked kindly.

"I am, thank you for asking."

He shrugged. "You're welcome. After all, you've let me invade your house."

"Well, Bill Reeger suggested that you would be a good public relations move."

Sean gulped. He hadn't really been concerned about generating goodwill for the family.

"You bet," he responded quietly. "Can I get you anything or do anything for you?"

She shook her head. "No thanks."

"Would you like to talk about it?"

She shrugged. "What's there to talk about?"

"How you're coping."

CHAPTER TWO

A sheen of tears appeared in her eyes like a light fog over the ground. "A lot of prayer."

"That's good that it gets you through. If you believe God is with you, that's a blessing."

"I know He is."

"No doubts?"

"Beyond the shadow of a doubt."

"You also have your Aunt Nancy."

"Yes, she's been like a second mother to me."

"What happened to your real mother?"

"She died when I was seven."

"I'm sorry." He was sorry for her, even though he realized that would be a great tidbit to add for human interest.

"It's okay. I'll see her again." Noting Sean's puzzled look, Esmerelda explained, "She's in heaven because she believed that Jesus saved her from her sin. I believe too. When I die, I'll be in heaven with her—and with Him."

"But not your dad?"

She shook her head. "No. Not unless he accepts Jesus as his Savior. My mother prayed for my dad all the time. Before she died, she pleaded with him to get saved. After she passed away, Dad grew angry against God. There was a change in him. I can't blame mom's death for what he did, but he grew angry and bitter after that, and this is what it led to."

NEW CREATION

She dropped her elbow on the table and put her head into her hands. Sobs shook her body. Sean got up and went to her chair. He knelt down and took her hand in his.

"It's okay to cry."

"I never cry, though," she admitted, some of the Dutch pride at self-contained emotion slipping through.

"You must have cried when your mother died?"

"Yes, I did. But that was so traumatic, nothing in my life seemed so bad after that."

He gently wiped a tear off her cheek. "I think this qualifies."

She sighed. "You're right." She hiccupped as the tears stopped. "Thank you for the encouragement."

Sean looked into her eyes, seeing a mix of quiet strength and vulnerability. "You're welcome. Tell you what, I need a break from what I'm doing, and you're not eating, why don't we discuss economic policies?"

"Good. You need to have your mind changed," she grinned.

Sean smiled back.

Later that afternoon, back at his place, Sean struggled to write his column. He had always been proud of his ability to write for hours on end, the fruitful appendages of his hands obliging in their servitude to his fertile mind. But today the words just wouldn't come. He tapped his fingers gently on the keys, watch-

CHAPTER TWO

ing the asdfasdfasdf show up on the screen. He backspaced and this time tapped jkl;jkl;jkl;. Sighing, he deleted this nonsense and put his hands behind his head and let his fingers run through his short, wiry brown hair.

His mind kept going back to Esmerelda. He'd met a lot of women, but Esmerelda was one of a kind. She was intelligent, yet beautiful. Kind, yet funny. Tender, yet rational. For a man who prized rational and critical thinking, Sean was hardly ever bested in a conversation when discussing politics or religion with the female gender. But Esmerelda had out-argued him—twice! He got up from his desk, knowing he wouldn't be getting any writing done yet. He pulled a beer from his fridge and went to lie down on the couch and watch a ball game. It didn't matter which one, just anything to get his mind off of his introspection.

But Sean ended up letting his mind wander as the game played. Whenever he left Esmerelda's house, he felt like a condemned felon, a criminal. He wasn't. He didn't do anything illegal. He looked at the Budweiser label on the brown bottle. He wasn't a drunk. He wasn't a pathological liar, he just told little white lies to keep himself out of trouble. If there were a heaven, would his good deeds outweigh his bad? That would be horrible if he had just one more bad deed than good.

For some reason, the theme "one was too much" drifted through his consciousness. Snatches of a Bible verse came to his mind, but he couldn't remember the whole thing. He'd heard some children at the church saying it. Something about the whole law. He got up and picked up his cell phone.

NEW CREATION

Esmerelda was sitting in her room at her vanity when the cell phone rang. She got up and walked over to where it was charging.

"Hello."

"Hi, Esmerelda. This is Sean Wallace."

"Hi. What can I do for you? I normally don't give interviews this late in the afternoon," there was a touch of humor in her voice.

"That's not what I need. I need a Bible verse."

"Just one?" she asked, and now he could hear a full-blown smile.

He chuckled. "For right now. What was that verse I heard yesterday about the whole law? Some of the kids clubbers were reciting it."

"'For whoever shall keep the whole law and yet stumble in one point, he is guilty of all.' James 2:10."

"That's the one. What does it mean?"

"It means that even if we follow all the commandments, but break just one, we're as guilty as if we had committed each one."

"That's the problem with your God," Sean replied darkly. "Too many don'ts."

"Why are you mad at all the don'ts?"

"Well, a person should do whatever they want."

"My dad did."

She had gotten him there. "I mean, within the law."

"Well, the law *is* don'ts. Isn't it? Don't go faster than 25 in a school zone. Don't murder. Don't steal. Don't forget to file your

CHAPTER TWO

income taxes before April 15th. The law is healthy. Otherwise, there would be anarchy and disorder, confusion and chaos."

Sean sighed. "Well, okay. Granted, some laws are good. But your God is a killjoy."

"Really? You think so? The God who created everything, including green grass, mountains, streams, oceans. People. Animals. Sex."

"What?" Sean laughed. "God created sex? You aren't serious, are you?"

"Where do you think it came from?"

Sean hadn't thought of that. "But God puts so many don'ts on it."

"Like don't keep your body from your spouse?"

"That's not in the Bible!"

"Sure it is. By the way, read Song of Solomon."

"I'll have to do that once I get a Bible."

"I have an extra one for you."

"Figures you would, Little Miss Goody-Two Shoes. But that doesn't erase all the other don'ts."

"What really bothers you about them?"

Sean was quiet. He knew he had to be honest with himself and honest with Esmerelda. Finally he answered. "Well, why tell us not to do things that all of us do and can't help from doing?"

"That's exactly right."

NEW CREATION

"What do you mean?" he asked, surprised at her agreement with him.

"That's why God gave us the law. To show us that we can't follow it. The failings to keep the laws are what sin is. He gave the law to show us that in order to get to heaven, we need to be redeemed from sin by one who never sinned. It's all explained in Galatians."

"Oh." It was actually starting to make sense. "That's why Adam and Eve's sin was so bad. It affects everyone and makes it so we can't help but choose sin."

"Right. That's in Romans."

He chuckled. "Let me guess, Jesus is the only perfect man," he kidded.

She was serious. "Correct. And since a man had to die for men, Jesus had to be born."

"So, the sin nature goes through the father."

"Correct."

"But Jesus was born without a father. I remember that from St. Agnes's Catholic Church."

"Yes. But Mary was a sinful human, Christ wasn't. Because He needed to rise again to show that God had accepted His sacrifice of dying on the cross, the Substitute itself needed to be God as well. Only God can give life. And guess who was fully God and fully man. Jesus. It is difficult to understand," she admitted.

"Although, that's the first time it's ever made sense," Sean remarked.

CHAPTER TWO

"See, the Spirit is opening your eyes."

"Really?" that seemed hard to believe, but his heart was warmed.

"Yes. I'll keep praying for you. Did you have any other questions?"

"Nope, and I have a lot to think about."

Sean hung up and sat down to write.

Van Heeder Arraigned for Embezzlement Case. Sean pounded on the keys as the words flowed quickly from his mind, his fingers struggling to keep up. *Objectivity is the goal,* he repeated to himself over and over in his mind. It was difficult to think of Van Heeder as a greedy capitalist without hearing Esmerelda's voice in his head: "If we break just one commandment, we're as guilty as if we had committed each one." That left a bad taste in Sean's mouth.

Despite being a "truth is what you make it" follower, he had his own set of absolutes. Intolerance was bad, so was judging, so was ... he stopped his train of thought to really dissect it. He was intolerant of Christians. He judged them harshly if he found a scrap of supposed hypocrisy. Apparently he was the hypocrite. He typed faster, hoping to drown out the warring voices in his head.

He'd been right ... his life would never be the same after this.

CHAPTER THREE

Genesis 1:9, 11a "*Then God said, 'Let the waters under the heavens be gathered together into one place, and let the dry land appear;' and it was so. Then God said, "Let the earth bring forth grass, the herb that yields seed, and the fruit tree that yields fruit according to its kind'."*

Esmerelda woke on Friday and turned to look at the clock. She groaned and pulled the covers over her head. The last few days had been so emotionally draining, she didn't want to get out of bed. She wondered where the light at the end of the tunnel was. She was eating breakfast when her Uncle Jarrod phoned her.

"Hi, Essie. I've got a deposition with your father today."

"May I come?"

"No. But I'm going to tell him that I want to do a plea bargain. If he admits

NEW CREATION

to it, he may get a reduced sentence. I'm just worried about the time it would take to get to trial, and all that money, mental, and emotional toll."

"If I can help at all, let me know."

"I will. Aunt Nancy has some errands to run, but she may head over to your place after that."

"Okay. Thanks, Uncle Jarrod."

His voice was tired. "You're welcome. I'll see you later."

Esmerelda hung up the phone and heard a car in the driveway. She looked out the window and, seeing Sean, gave a sigh of weariness. She had agreed to Sean's constant shadow as a necessary evil and used the discussions with him to get her mind off of her father's upcoming trial and likely jail sentence. But knowing that her every step was closely watched for inconsistency and her actions eyeballed for hypocrisy set her on edge.

Sean set down his laptop on the dinner table across from Esmerelda as she finished her bowl of cereal.

"No eggs and toast?" he asked.

She shook her head. "We don't have a cook anymore."

"Can you cook?"

"I probably could learn. How hard is it to follow a recipe?"

"Not too hard. I've lived off my own cooking for a decade."

"Oh."

Sean noticed her non-committal attitude. He started tapping away.

CHAPTER THREE

"About what are you writing?"

"Another trial that's going on," he answered truthfully.

"Oh."

The phone rang and Esmerelda went to answer it. Sean listened to the conversation.

"Hello. Yes, this is she. Oh, hello, Mr. Arbondnut. How are you? I'm fine." She listened for a few seconds. Sean watched her face as it fell and as she struggled for control. But there were no tears and no anger portrayed on those lovely features.

"I understand. It's okay, I'll be fine. How long do I have until I have to be out?"

She bit her lip as she listened. "Thirty days. That's very generous of you. Thank you so much for your graciousness in all of this. Do you have a buyer? No? So I should go ahead with the estate sale?"

Pacing, she listened. She stopped when she spoke. "Well, I'm not selling personal items or anything I inherited from my mother. I don't care about the cars or the furniture."

More pacing.

Pause. "I'll start packing as soon as possible. Yes, thank you."

She hung up the phone and Sean noticed a slight tremble in her hands. He got up and went into the kitchen to get her a drink. There were gadgets he would never be rich enough to afford, stainless steel appliances that were top of the line. He reached for a glass and filled it with water and brought it out to her. He led her to a chair.

NEW CREATION

"Here you go."

"Thank you," she whispered.

Sean patted her back. "You're going to be fine."

"I know. I have to call Aunt Nancy and purchase cardboard boxes for packing … find a place to live."

"It's okay to cry about it."

"About what?"

"Losing your home."

"Maybe I will later. But it's going to go to pay the debt that we owe to the people dad robbed. That makes me feel better."

"*You* don't owe it. He does. You're innocent. I've made that clear in my articles."

Esmerelda nodded. "I know, but his sin affects me, too." After a bit she looked up at him. "You know, there's a song that I used to sing in youth group. She started singing quietly. *'He paid a debt He did not owe, I owed a debt I could not pay, I needed someone to wash my sins away. And now I sing a brand new song, amazing grace, all day long. Christ Jesus paid a debt that I could never pay.'* Jesus was innocent, too, you know. But he died to pay the debt of your sin."

Sean gulped. "You think that if it will help, but don't try to convert me," he snapped and walked over to his computer. He had to write about the estate sale and the bank taking over the house. This was big. He doubted any other newspapers had this knowledge. Within moments, attention to his job kept him from thinking on Esmerelda's words.

CHAPTER THREE

Esmerelda watched him type and prayed for him. God must be convicting him for him to get so upset about the knowledge of his sin and Christ's sacrifice. After a few moments, Sean looked up.

"I'll take you to buy cardboard boxes if you'd like."

"Maybe we should wait until Aunt Nancy gets here."

"All right. When she's here and I'm finished with this column, we'll go buy packing boxes. Good thing I'm here to do the heavy lifting."

Her smile was kind. "It's why I let you in the door this morning."

While they waited for Esmerelda's aunt, Sean paced restlessly, as Esmerelda looked out the window, perfectly still, and looking at peace.

"What catches your attention?" Sean asked.

"The loveliness of the trees in the drizzle."

He looked out. It was a pretty sight. He sighed. "It's just sad how much the earth sorrows because of all the people. Our capitalist society is killing the trees and the animals."

He heard her chuckle and turned to her. "Don't you care?"

"I care about the earth, but it's not humans' fault. You would have everyone believe that if there were no people, the earth would be returned to its splendor."

NEW CREATION

"Well, it would." Great, now she was going to argue environmentalism.

"You think that it's better in the primitive jungles? You would have people return to the pre-industrial revolution days out of a mistaken belief that humans are the problem?"

He shrugged. "Well, think of all the pollution and all the trees dying. Because there's so much private property and so many corporations, it's difficult to regulate what goes on with nature."

"Tell me something, Sean, have you ever lived somewhere with a yard?"

"Oh yeah."

"Whose yard do you care most about, yours or a person across town?"

"Mine." *Duh*, he finished in his head.

"So, if you needed to chop down a tree for wood for a fire, and it had to come from your yard or the person across town, in which case would you be more motivated to replant?"

"If the tree came from my yard."

"Why?"

He hated the dead end she'd led him down, and nearly ground through his teeth, "Because it's my yard, I want to have shade and I like trees."

"Exactly. If you look at places where people don't own the resources they use, there's no motivation to take care of them. Sure, there are industries here, but the competitive nature of capitalism weeds out the practices that are the most destructive. And really,

CHAPTER THREE

would you like to return to a primitive society where you're lucky to just survive?"

He sighed, thinking of his A/C and heat and electric blanket. "No."

"God created the world and put man in charge as a steward, not to abuse the earth but to put it to its best use. That does mean replanting trees and being wise in the use of its resources, but mankind is not the problem."

Sean didn't feel like arguing more—and probably losing again—so he changed the subject, thankful that Nancy was finally arriving.

When Nancy came in, she immediately burst into tears. Sean was trying to remember a time in the short few days he'd known her that she wasn't crying. Esmerelda held her kindly and let her cry. Finally, she untangled the older woman from her arms.

"Okay, Aunt Nancy. I've got to go buy boxes to pack things in."

"Are you going with him?" Nancy asked.

Sean sighed. "Tell you what. I'll go buy the boxes myself, you can stay here and get ready to pack. How many do you think you need?"

Esmerelda gave him a number and he left. When he returned, Esmerelda and Aunt Nancy had already finished wrapping the knick-knacks in the living room.

Sean watched them for a few minutes. Aunt Nancy was still wiping tears from her eyes, but Esmerelda's face was composed.

NEW CREATION

Often Nancy would hold up something and would tearfully remind Esmerelda where it came from.

"I remember when your mother... " or "Do you remember when your Dad...."

Esmerelda would nod and laugh or smile.

"It's okay, Aunt Nancy," she kept reminding her. "Mom left me more than just these things. She's the one that led me to Christ."

Aunt Nancy didn't seem to understand why that mattered.

"But she'd be so sad to see this house being sold. She loved this house."

"She has a mansion in heaven, Aunt Nancy."

Or a little later, "Oh, and the Monet print. Such a beautiful scene. Now it must be sold," and Nancy shed more tears.

Esmerelda stood and put her hand on her lower back. "Aunt Nancy," she said firmly. "My mother doesn't need Monet. She is looking on the face of God."

Sean pondered all this. Nancy was an ocean of tears. Esmerelda's eyes were dry as dust; the tears she had shed yesterday were gone. Sean didn't know how he would deal with a tragedy like this, but he doubted he'd go through it with the grace that Esmerelda possessed. She had a foundation that her aunt didn't have. That Sean didn't have. Sean watched the young woman box up the things she was keeping, and he couldn't begin to calculate the amount of money originally spent on the things she was leaving behind. There was something more important than what she

CHAPTER THREE

owned. Something within her. Her position with God. Her character. Her hope for a future better than the present.

Sean looked out the window. There was a brief interlude from the rain. The sun was hitting the trees. The blue sky stretched toward the lake. But Sean was aware that underneath the blue sky and the yellow sun were myriads of crimes, tears, sorrow. The earth was beautiful but it contained a depth of evil that even Sean couldn't fathom. And Sean knew that his life was the same way. Behind the smiling, polite façade he liked to show to people, he was as evil as the next person. As evil as Van Heeder. For a long time, he'd been so angry at people who didn't get involved in environmental issues. Now that seemed insignificant to the real problem—man's heart. He had never considered it before, but for some reason, it was clear to him.

Sean turned around and noticed Esmerelda taping up the first box. He stepped forward. "Here, where do you want me to take that?"

"Just set it by the door."

It took the rest of the day to pack the house. Esmerelda was leaving almost everything. She had set a box inside her father's study, but hadn't gone in to pack it yet.

Sean took a break in the afternoon to write his article.

Van Heeder's Daughter Sells Estate to Pay Debt.

This was a big break for the *Daily Gazette,* Sean knew it. So far, none of the other papers had gotten a whiff of what Esmerelda

NEW CREATION

was doing. They were still focusing on the arraignment. Sean could not wait to break this story. He thought of the kudos he'd get from his boss and the possible monetary and promotional blessings and smiled. He felt his spirits lift. Let Esmerelda say what she wanted, life didn't get any better than reaching the top. He finished the article and logged into his webmail to e-mail it to Vance. There was an e-mail in his inbox from the HR department at his office. He opened it and saw the official e-mail announcing the layoffs of three of Sean's co-workers. Sean's good mood hit the earth with a thud and mixed with a fear for his job and a relief that, for right now, he still had it. He also admired, once again, Esmerelda's strength in the midst of adversity. Maybe she really did know what she was talking about. After all, she'd been right about many things.

Sean packed up his stuff and went back to stacking boxes by the front door. He headed upstairs to find Esmerelda and Aunt Nancy in Esmerelda's room. Sean looked around the bedroom and bathroom suite. It was larger than his apartment. His attention turned back to the women.

Esmerelda was pulling things out of the closet and making a pile on the bed. For some reason, Aunt Nancy was not happy about this. Did he detect a sheen of tears in the older woman's eyes? No, impossible! Would this make Aunt Nancy cry, too?

"Esmerelda, you're making a big mistake. This is expensive clothing. Why, look at this purse. It probably cost about $1,000."

"So what. I have too many purses."

"What's going on?" Sean asked.

CHAPTER THREE

Esmerelda and Aunt Nancy looked at him. Aunt Nancy pleaded with him.

"Sean, see if you can talk to her. She wants to donate all these things to Goodwill or the Salvation Army."

Sean raised his eyebrows. "Really?"

"Yes, it's just ridiculous. These are expensive clothes she's just giving away. She could at least sell them."

Sean looked at Esmerelda and she shook her head. "I could, but there's no reason why I should try to sell them when I could give them away and let someone have perfectly good clothes for a bargain price."

Sean, who believed in wealth redistribution—or had believed in wealth redistribution—was ashamed that he'd never once thought about helping out in such a simple way. He owned clothes he could give away.

"Do you want me to drop those off at the Salvation Army on my way home?" he asked.

Esmerelda smiled at him. "Thank you, Sean, I would."

Even though the Salvation Army drop-off center was south in Evanston, and Sean lived west of the Van Heeder's, Sean went home first. He had a couple of old suits he never wore. He could drop those off as well. Maybe that would assuage his guilt.

CHAPTER FOUR

Genesis 1:14a "Then God said, 'Let there be lights in the firmament of the heavens to divide the day from the night'."

*S*ean didn't know what to do with his Saturday that week. He'd been on the go for several days working almost non-stop on the Van Heeder story. When he wasn't writing it, he was gathering information for the article. He also realized that it was one of the first weekends he had woken up without a splitting headache from a hangover.

He threw off the covers and stepped out of bed onto the hard wooden floor. He stood and went over to the window. Looking through the blinds, he noticed it was raining again, no doubt a consequence of the hurricanes in the Gulf of Mexico. Oh, what he would give for a sunny day that lasted.

After dressing and eating a bowl of cereal, he sat down at his computer but

NEW CREATION

didn't write anything. He finally closed the lid of his notebook computer and stood up. He grabbed his keys and stuck his wallet in his back pocket and left the apartment. He wasn't sure where to go that day, or what to do, but something seemed to be calling him to go see Esmerelda.

He drove to her house and rang the doorbell. After a few brief minutes, she opened the door. Even though she wore jogging pants and an old United City Bank T-shirt, she still looked attractive.

"Sean?"

"Hi, I wondered if you needed company."

"No thank you, Sean," she replied properly. "I'm just going to be alone today."

"I finished some of your books. Do you want to talk about them?"

Esmerelda sighed, the first sign that maybe she wasn't all that pleased to see him. "Why not? Come on in. Now, is this for your column?"

Sean shook his head. "This is completely off the record," he replied honestly. "Look, I don't even have my computer with me today."

"How comforting. I thought perhaps you'd had it surgically attached to your side," she grinned.

"Nope. Can't be any more attached than you are with your Bible."

CHAPTER FOUR

Her laughter rang out. "What a compliment, thank you, Sean."

He smiled. She fascinated him with her resilience. It seemed as though nothing could get her down.

"Oh look," she suddenly said. "It looks like the rain has lessened. The sun's coming out."

Sean looked. Sure enough, the clouds were parting. Maybe it would last.

"We could take some chairs out to the patio and sit out there," she suggested.

"Sure."

"Or take a walk. I would like to get out of the house, it's been a bit cloistering in here."

"Sure. There's got to be a park we can walk at."

She grabbed her jacket and headed out to his car. He opened her door. She looked surprised at his polite gesture.

"Thank you."

"You're most welcome, my lady."

She chuckled. "I'm hardly nobility."

He grinned at her as he climbed in. He couldn't explain to her the air she presented. He'd often wondered what it meant when someone was honorable. Looking at her, now he knew. He remembered a boring sermon from St. Agnes's church when he was a boy. He couldn't recall the whole sermon, but he clearly

NEW CREATION

remembered the verse the priest had read: "Who can find a virtuous wife? For her worth is far above rubies."

The verse had stuck with Sean as a young boy, thinking how awesome it would be to find buried treasure and wondering how a woman could be better than that. The priest had gone on in sonorous tones to relate the verse to the virgin Mary, whereupon Sean had stopped listening. Sean glanced at Esmerelda gazing out the window as he drove through the streets toward Gilson Park. She was a virtuous woman, and though her worth may be above rubies, the price to get her would take more than Sean was ready to give.

"So, have you finished packing your dad's things?" he asked.

She nodded. "Pretty much. Hey, can I change the station?"

He sighed. Apparently she didn't like hip-hop. "Okay."

She turned to a classical station. They pulled up to a quiet preserve and started ambling down the path. They were silent for a few minutes. Esmerelda eventually broke the silence.

"So, what did you want to talk about?"

"Well, I read through several of your books and they had very good logical arguments. Although, I don't know if you can use the Bible as a backup for an argument."

With a voice slightly tinged with sarcasm, Esmerelda said "Right, using books written by men who could never know everything rather than a book written by an omniscient God."

"Yeah, but ... the Bible. I mean, it's so full of holes."

CHAPTER FOUR

"Name one book that has no problems."

Silence met her command.

"Sean, Sean, the Bible is the word of God. It is truth. There are no holes and no problems like man's writings. If it looks like there's a problem between the Bible and your thinking, change your thinking."

"I can barely understand the Bible."

"You're not saved. It's God's letter written to the bride of His Son, His children. If you're not a child of God, you're not going to understand it."

"And there is where you try to save my immortal soul," he quipped, hiding his annoyance.

"I can only pray for you. God has to save your soul."

"Why do you care?"

"Because hell is not the place you want to end up. Have you ever had a day when you hadn't eaten all day, and your stomach was craving food?"

"Yeah."

"I could imagine that that might be what hell is like, along with the continual fire, that starving feeling that consumes your being even though you know you'll never get fed."

"Stop it, okay," he cut her off harshly.

Esmerelda knew the Spirit and the Devil were fighting for Sean's soul and she went silent, praying for him.

NEW CREATION

After a few moments of silence, "Are you talking to God about me?" he asked without spite but with a tinge of humor.

"Yes, I am."

"Thank you," he whispered.

"You're welcome."

They kept walking, making their way around puddles as the sun brightened, warming them in its late summer rays.

"As a journalist, I'm used to researching arguments, and I would have to say that creation would be the most consistent beginning to this world. Doing the columns on your dad has legal terminology on my brain, and God seems to have put things in motion in a very legal way. I mean, guilt, punishment, justification, etcetera."

"Exactly. God is just, and there would be no foundation for his justice if He hadn't created a world of order."

"Gives a whole new meaning to the term natural laws, doesn't it."

She smiled up at him, eyes bright. "Very good observation, Sean. I think God is opening up truths to you."

"Not many."

"For now, they're like stars beginning to shine from the night sky. You don't see them all at once, but if you keep gazing to the heavens, they brighten as you watch."

He grinned at her. "That's very poetic."

"Thanks."

CHAPTER FOUR

"Do you write?"

"No," she laughed with embarrassment. "I mean, a little bit, yes. Nothing big. Just my thoughts on things."

"You ever thought of being a journalist?"

She shook her head, her curls bouncing around her face in such a feminine way, that Sean wished that he could push them back from her face. He kept his hands in his pockets and asked her "Why not?"

She answered him with a touch of humor in her eyes. "I couldn't even begin to pretend to be objective."

He laughed out loud. They kept walking. The sun warmed them, but the smell of earthworms and stagnant water assailed their nostrils.

"If the clouds stay away, perhaps tonight I'll get to see the moon. It should be almost a full moon," she mentioned.

"You like to look at the moon?"

"I do. I love to stare up at the moon."

"You're a fascinating woman, Essie." He informed her, using her nickname for the first time. "Tell me, what do you like about the moon?"

"The crags and craters of its features, and the beauty of its stark face. The fact that we always just see the one side," her voice was intense and passionate. "How it works upon the earth to create the tides. Have you ever studied how important the tides are?"

"No, I haven't, but if remember anything from fourth grade earth science, they are important, aren't they?"

NEW CREATION

She nodded. "They keep the ocean from stagnating."

"Well, the moon is pretty impressive."

She nodded and looked up at him, a far-away look in her eyes. "My goal is to be like the moon; its whole purpose is to reflect the sun."

For a second he didn't understand her meaning. But words from a few minutes ago came back to him, mixed with the basic catechism of the church.

"You mean, Jesus, don't you? The Son of God."

She nodded. Her features were soft, and her eyes were still focused on something far away. They continued to walk in silence before finally deciding to turn around and leisurely head to the car. Sean bought them food from a drive-thru, surprised and pleased that Esmerelda devoured a burger and fries instead of picking at a salad. He dropped her off and walked her up to the door.

"Thank you for lunch, Sean."

"Sure. Make sure you relax some today."

"I will."

He walked back to his car and then turned.

"Essie," he called.

She was halfway through the door when he stopped her. She turned around.

"Yes?"

"You make a wonderful moon."

With that, he climbed into his car and sped off.

CHAPTER FIVE

Genesis 1:20 "Then God said, 'Let the waters abound with an abundance of living creatures, and let birds fly above the earth across the face of the firmament of the heavens.'"

Sean paced the small expanse of his living/dining/kitchen area in his apartment. He fingered the ripped edge of the slip of paper he held in his hand and read again the address he had memorized.

The day before, Essie had invited him to church and then to lunch afterward at her house. Church did not sound so inviting, but that was the condition of getting a home-cooked meal. Since he didn't know anyone else who was cooking a Sunday dinner for him, he finally gave in and went down to his car. He'd been to her church on Wednesday night, so he had a vague idea of where it was located.

NEW CREATION

He found it and pulled up next to a car that looked quite a bit like the Perrys'. He started sketching the next day's column in his mind about the religious affiliation of Van Heeder's sister, brother-in-law and daughter. But he forgot to continue with the mental draft as he entered the church.

Sean felt like an interloper and couldn't stop the relief that engulfed him when he saw Essie waiting by the sanctuary doors. She lit up when she saw him and made her way over.

Sean forced his gaze from wandering lower than her eyes; he was in a church after all. She was wearing a flared navy blue skirt, and her ivory, cashmere, button-up sweater lay on her slender frame so perfectly. She was wearing nylons and navy dress shoes. Pearls—most likely her mother's—encircled her fair, delicate throat. Sean had forgotten how enticing women could look in modest skirts. Nothing above her knees or more than two inches below her neck showed, but the way the hem of her skirt swished around her knees when she walked caused him to firmly reel his imagination away from a place he did not think God would appreciate finding it. He swallowed, ashamed of himself for thinking such things on a Sunday.

She came up to him and gently flipped a lock of hair behind her shoulder driving him wild with desire. Oh, the untouchable ones, they were always the ones worth having. She was completely unaware of this as she smiled up at him, her blue eyes bright with pleasure at seeing him there.

"Sean, you came! Come on in. We're ready to start."

CHAPTER FIVE

He followed her into the sanctuary and into a row where Nancy and Jarrod sat. They didn't look too happy to see him, but they didn't say anything. The congregation was standing to start the first song when Esmerelda and Sean slipped into the pew, so there was no time to talk before the service started.

Sean enjoyed the singing, but the sermon was mostly lost on him. At the end, the pastor implored the unsaved people in the congregation to follow Christ. Sean knew Essie was concerned about his eternity, but he knew what getting saved meant — it meant a different life, and he liked the one he had.

"Your life has always been easy," a still, small voice spoke to him as the congregation sang "Just As I Am." He tried to push the voice away, but it wouldn't go. *"What were to happen to you if you lost your money, house, job, and family? Would you handle it like Esmerelda?"*

Sean knew the answer was no. He glanced at Esmerelda who had her eyes closed as she sang. She'd had everything of value taken from her, and yet, she had everything of worth still with her. It was a strange dichotomy. Things that mattered very much on earth were lost to her, but she had a Heavenly Father. Sean gulped and felt tears begin to sting his eyes. He was there to write articles about her earthly father's troubles, and the more he learned about her earthly father, the more she taught him about her Heavenly Father. God.

The Creator of the universe was her Father.

The song ended, and Sean quickly blinked to dispel the slight sheen of moisture. He was a hardened journalist; where had the emotion come from?

NEW CREATION

"*I created you with emotions, and I'm tugging at them just as I'm tugging at your mind,*" the voice spoke to him.

Sean was beginning to believe that it was God speaking to him. Or perhaps it was the Spirit. He remembered his prayer just a few days ago that the Spirit would open his eyes. Had his prayer truly been answered? He hadn't believed it could happen when he prayed it. But apparently, God didn't plan His works around humans' wants.

Esmerelda put her hand on his arm, startling him back to reality. He looked down at her.

"Ready to go get lunch?" she asked sweetly.

He nodded and moved out of the pew. He followed the Perrys to Esmerelda's house. He went inside and found that the dining room was all set up.

Dinner wasn't quite ready, so Sean sat with Nancy and Jarrod in the living room while Esmerelda finished the last preparations. There wasn't much to say and the atmosphere was tense. It was obvious that Jarrod did not approve of Sean as a friend, and just barely accepted him as a journalist, so Sean tried to keep the topic on things that wouldn't stir controversy. They talked about the Cubs being the top team in the division until Esmerelda finally called them for lunch.

"I'm keeping my grandmother's dishes and linens," Esmerelda explained as she poured water in the glasses.

Nancy sighed as she looked at the expensive china and crystal arrayed on the table. "Did you have to unpack them, Dear?"

CHAPTER FIVE

"Yes, but I can just as easily pack them again. This is a special occasion."

They sat down at the table as Esmerelda brought out the salad and tureen of soup. Sean's mouth watered at the buttery rolls she brought out. Finally she brought out the salmon.
"My dad loves salmon and it's one of the only things I know how to make," Esmerelda admitted.

Sean couldn't wait to take a bite, but he waited until after Esmerelda prayed before digging his fork into the tender flesh. It had been marinated in something, but Sean had no idea what, and Esmerelda wouldn't give the secret away.

"This is delicious," Jarrod said.

"I agree," Sean replied, "It was very kind of you to have me over to dinner today."

She smiled. "I didn't mind."

"You used it as bait though to get me to church, didn't you?" Sean asked.

She grinned and nodded. "I did. God calls his disciples to be fishers of men, so that's what I'm doing. Did you enjoy the service?"

Jarrod patted his lips with his napkin. "It was the typical condemning sort of sermon that I've heard before."

"For God did not send His Son into the world to condemn the world, but that the world through Him might be saved.

"He who believes in Him is not condemned; but he who does not believe is condemned already, because he has not believed

NEW CREATION

in the name of the only begotten Son of God," she quipped in answer.

"Is that in the Bible?" Sean asked, amazed at her ability to quote Scripture.

She nodded. "Yes, John 3:17-18."

Jarrod did not seem pleased. "I thought God was a God of love."

"He is, Uncle Jarrod. In verse 16 it says, 'For God so loved the world that He gave His only begotten Son, that whoever believes in Him should not perish but have everlasting life.' You have to have the bad news and the good news, Uncle Jarrod. What if you were to have an innocent client and after walking into the courtroom the judge were to pronounce him innocent and set him free."

"I'd be pleased," Jarrod responded. "But I would expect it if he truly were innocent."

"All right, well, what if you were to go into the courtroom with Dad in a few days, and the judge were to tell you that he was letting Dad free because Mr. Arbondnut at the bank had taken the punishment and jail time and paid off all the creditors."

Jarrod cocked his head in puzzlement. "What are you getting at?"

"Every human is born with a sin nature, Uncle Jarrod, and we choose to sin. And when we sin, we sin against God and His Son, because he created us and He is holy and without sin. But Jesus came down to earth as a man and died on the cross. He was the one wronged, but He took our sins and paid the punishment.

CHAPTER FIVE

He is our substitute, and when God saw the price Jesus paid, His justice was satisfied.

"Think of that, Uncle Jarrod. The great Judge of all the earth was satisfied with the sacrifice of His Son for all time. If you only believe that Jesus died on the cross for your sins and that He rose again, your sins will be forgiven. It's not living a good life, because we'll never be perfect. I struggle all the time with pride and worry. It's not going to church, because that doesn't make us righteous. It's accepting the free gift of salvation."

The table was quiet as Esmerelda finished her impassioned plea. Sean's eyes were riveted to her face as she poured out her heart to her uncle. He'd never heard such an invitation to be saved, and he'd never felt such a strong tug on his mind and heart. Everything she said had been seared into his brain. He knew that the words would prick him for a long time afterward. According to what she said, if he died, he would end up in hell. From what he remembered learning about hell, it was a lake of fire. He wondered if indeed people there lived in a constant state of physical, emotional, and spiritual starvation.

Jarrod didn't answer his niece, but instead turned the conversation to different things. Dinner passed slowly. When they finished, Jarrod and Nancy took their leave. They both kissed Esmerelda's forehead, but nothing was said about her words at the beginning of the dinner. Sean took off his sport coat and helped her clear the table.

"So, tell me, what happens if you get saved and then decide that you don't want to be saved?" he asked as he piled the plates and utensils by the sink.

NEW CREATION

She took out some Tupperware containers and started storing the food.

"When you trust Christ as your Savior, God sends the Holy Spirit as a seal, a promise of the eternal life in Heaven that is yours when you trust Christ."

"So, what does the Holy Spirit do?"

"The Holy Spirit comforts believers, convicts them of their sin, and holds back the corruption in the world. He also opens the eyes of sinners so that they can be saved, and lifts up Jesus."

"Ah. Sounds like a big job."

"The Holy Spirit is God, so He can handle it."

"All these Gods," Sean sighed as he opened the dishwasher and started loading it.

"There is one God, but He is three persons. Each of them is as much God in themselves. It's called the Trinity. They have different roles, but they're all equal. They were all present at Jesus' baptism. There was God speaking from Heaven, Jesus being baptized, and the Spirit descending like a dove."

"Like a dove?"

"Yes, I have to admit, I'm not exactly sure why like a dove. Unless it's because the dove stands for peace, and if we have the Holy Spirit dwelling in us we have peace with God." She paused as she thought about this, her lips pursed and forehead wrinkled in indecision.

Sean pounced at her seeming indecision. "See there, even you don't understand it. I like things that I can understand."

CHAPTER FIVE

"You would want a God you could understand?" Esmerelda asked.

Sean thought about this. "Well ... I don't know."

She opened the fridge to put the leftovers away. "If the attributes of God could be understood by human minds, He wouldn't be much of a God."

"I see your point."

"What's wrong, Sean? Why are you fighting so hard?"

Sean looked at her askance. "What makes you think I'm fighting?"

"Because you're a sinner; you belong to the Devil and he doesn't want to let you go. So you try to hide behind caustic comments and pretend it's God's fault for not being more 'understandable.'"

"What makes you say I belong to the Devil?"

She closed the fridge. "Because if you don't belong to God, then you belong to the Devil."

Sean absolutely did not like the idea that he belonged to the Devil. Did not like it one bit. Her words also put the kibosh on his rebuttal that he liked his life how it was. If it were true and the Devil was his master, it didn't matter how Sean lived. His soul was lost for eternity. He gulped.

"But what about if you sin really bad after being saved? Will God take away your salvation?"

Esmerelda softened. "No, Sean. If you're truly saved, you can never lose that. People who walk away from salvation are

NEW CREATION

backslidden, which means they do have eternal life, but not the blessings in this one. Or, they were never saved in the first place. Remember, nothing you do will bring you eternal life, so nothing you do can make you lose eternal life."

Sean's heart warmed a bit. He looked at the clock on the oven and grimaced.

"I know this might sound like I'm cutting and running, but I have to go. I usually have to call my mom on Sunday afternoons. If I don't, she gets worried about her 'little boy.'"

"Don't worry about it. I understand. Be thankful you have a mother, and make sure that you tell her you love her."

Sean grinned as he grabbed his sport coat and started toward the door.

"Has anyone told you how bossy you are?" he asked. "You can add that to pride and worry."

She rolled her eyes. "Just go call your mom."

Sean laughed and made his way out the door.

That night, as Esmerelda lay in bed, she thought with a heavy heart over her lunch with her aunt, uncle, and Sean. She sensed that God was opening Sean's eyes and that he was close to salvation. She pleaded with God to save him. Her aunt and uncle had heard the gospel over and over, but they still made no move to accept it. She hoped that she wasn't a stumbling block. She hoped she was genuine when talking with them about her own problems.

Her thoughts then turned to her father. He also had never made a choice to accept the free gift of salvation. He always

CHAPTER FIVE

worked so hard to make more money and was always proud of what he'd done. She hoped that perhaps now that he'd been humbled, God would shower him with grace.

Esmerelda's thoughts returned to Sean. Despite his liberal ideologies, his hardened attitude, and his wayward lifestyle, he was almost like a friend. She hadn't met many men who were as interesting as he was, and she hoped that even if she was in his life for only a little while that she could be the tool to bring him to Christ.

Daydreaming that Sean, her aunt, uncle, and father would find the freedom in the Lord she served, she fell asleep.

CHAPTER SIX

Genesis 1:24, 26a, 27 "Then God said, 'Let the earth bring forth the living creature according to its kind: cattle and creeping thing and beast of the earth, each according to its kind'; and it was so. Then God said, 'Let Us make man in Our image, according to Our likeness ... So God created man in His own image; in the image of God He created him; male and female He created them.'"

Esmerelda paced in the waiting room of the jail as her uncle talked with her father in another room. She heard someone clearing their throat and looked up.

"Oh, hello, Sean," she mumbled when he stepped into view.

"Your uncle in with your Dad?" he asked, wiping at the raindrops on his coat.

She nodded. "Yes, he's trying to get Dad to take the plea bargain."

NEW CREATION

Sean pulled out his notebook. "May I take notes?"

"Go ahead, I guess."

He flipped to a blank page and pulled out his pencil. "All right, what do you know?"

Esmerelda sighed. "Oh, you know the drill. Reduced sentence if he pleads guilty at the hearing or pre-trial or whatever it is that we have tomorrow. Uncle Jarrod says it could be a long time before we have the trial and if he's found guilty at that, it's more jail time. I understand where he's coming from to suggest taking a plea bargain."

"And what do you think about it?" Sean asked, as he scribbled away.

"I wish he'd plead guilty because he is guilty."

Sean's pen paused. As a journalist there were a lot of repercussions if he declared someone guilty before a jury found him guilty. A great story, but possible lawsuits. Sticky.

"Say again?"

"Just between you and me, Sean, he's guilty, and it's the right thing to do to admit when you're wrong."

Sean tried to frame a story.

Van Heeder's Lawyer pushes plea bargain. Daughter wants Truth. Tomorrow, Gregory Van Heeder will face the judge in the pre-trial conference for his alleged embezzlement of $3 million from United City Bank.

CHAPTER SIX

From there, all Sean could think of were gushing commendations of Esmerelda.

"Get a grip," he told himself. He was becoming far too besotted with the young woman.

It was hard not to be as she stood in an expensive brown pantsuit that flattered her figure. But despite the proper way she carried herself, she had the vulnerable air about her that tugged heavily on Sean's desire to protect.

"Do you think he will take the plea bargain?"

Esmerelda shrugged. "It's possible he will if only to get out of an extended sentence. He's still not apologetic or convicted about what he's done," she moaned.

Sean knew that bothered her most of all. "I'm sorry, Essie. I wish I could help."

"There is nothing you can do."

"Have you talked to your PR team recently?"

Essie shook her head. "Not too much. Since I offered to pay back the money, they've mostly been fielding phone calls."

"Ah. I see."

She sat down on a bench to wait, and he sat down next to her.

"You did a good job in the article breaking the restitution angle," she complimented him.

"Thanks."

She sighed. "I'm sorry I'm not very good company today," she murmured softly.

NEW CREATION

"It's okay. You're heartbroken over your father."

"It's difficult when one you love is a ... thief."

The last word came out in stark pain. Sean had been indifferent to Gregory's theft except as a way for him to get a great story, but now his anger flared up again seeing the hurt glimmering in Esmerelda's eyes. Anger not at her, but at her dad for ruining her life. She didn't show her emotions much in public, but Sean recognized that she was upset and heartbroken over what her father had done. No matter what she said, it was difficult watching everything in your life get taken from you.

He tried to think of something to say. "You know, life is a struggle, Esmerelda, and for millennia, people have done what they can to get ahead. Before a moral code was evolved with society, this wouldn't have been a big deal," he spouted off.

"If we were animals, there would be no moral code, Sean, and this would be the way of life. But we aren't, and we didn't evolve from animals. Which is why there *is* a moral code. It's created in us. Animals do what animals do, but it is mankind and humanity that functions within the boundaries of morality, values, and ethics. Without them, our society would be a mess. There are absolutes, and they're given to us by God. Which is why even people like you find what my father did shameful!"

Sean looked down at his notebook, wishing he had a rebuttal, but he didn't. He hadn't really even believed what he'd told her in the first place. In the last week, his convictions had been challenged, questioned, and debated, and they had not stood up to the test. It bothered him a bit, especially when he found he

CHAPTER SIX

wasn't as open-minded as he liked to think he was. Jarrod came down the hall just then and Esmerelda stood.

"Hello, Essie. Hello, Sean."

"Hello, Mr. Perry. How is Mr. Van Heeder? Is he doing well?"

Jarrod looked a bit surprised at Sean's concern but he nodded. "Yes, he's looking fine, a little bit wan, but that's to be expected."

Jarrod started for the door with Esmerelda and Sean following behind. Uncle and niece started discussing the case.

"I've talked to him about a plea bargain and what it would mean for him."

"Will he take it?" Essie asked. "What is the offer?"

"I can't divulge those facts to you, but if you can remember to pray for him, Essie, as I know you do already. He's breaking."

Essie stopped walking and her breath caught. "Oh, Uncle Jarrod, is he okay?" she asked, stricken.

"Yes, my dear. But facing jail time is a horrid thing for a man."

"I would take it for him, Uncle Jarrod. Would they let me go to jail for him?"

Sean gave Esmerelda a double take. Jarrod put his arm on Essie's shoulder. "No, my dear. You've done what you can, but I'm sure your father would be grateful for how much you care."

He picked up his umbrella and led her out the door.

NEW CREATION

That night, Sean tapped furiously on his keyboard as he finished the column he was working on. It was for a different article than the Van Heeder case, for which he was glad. Every time he thought about the Van Heeder case, he could still hear Essie's voice pleading with her uncle to take her father's punishment.

"I took your punishment," the small voice that had become a daily companion whispered.

Sean ignored it and put the last touches on the article and then proofread it. Finding it practically flawless, he sent it off to Vance. He, personally, was pleased with the amount of research he'd done, and the equal way he'd covered both sides of the story.

But with the article finished, it was time to turn to the Van Heeder case. He sighed and looked through the columns he'd already written. Tomorrow was the pre-trial conference. Sean was to meet Esmerelda at the courthouse at 9 a.m. He couldn't wait until the Van Heeder case was over. Then he would be free. Free from Esmerelda's impossible debates, free from the guilt-inducing questions, free from that blasted still, small voice that wouldn't let him sleep!

"Why can't you leave me alone?!" he shouted out loud, looking toward the ceiling.

"Why are you fighting so hard?" the question came in a soft whisper upon his spirit.

"Why did you pick me to bother with?" he answered with a growl, not feeling silly that he was arguing out loud with no one.

"Because I love you."

CHAPTER SIX

Sean plopped down on his sofa and dropped his head in hands. He closed his eyes, and pictured himself standing in a courtroom. He was the one on trial. He thought through the things he'd done that would probably count as sins.

"I died for those sins."

The silent voice wouldn't leave him alone. It was almost beginning to be real. He wondered if he were quiet enough if he'd actually hear it speaking to him audibly.

His eyes caught the Bible Esmerelda had loaned him. What had she called it? A letter to God's children. She'd told him that it was how God spoke to humans.

He picked it up and flipped it open. The Bible fell open to II Corinthians 5:17 "Therefore, if anyone is in Christ, he is a new creation; old things have passed away; behold, all things have become new."

A new creation. He flipped back to the beginning of the Bible and his eyes caught the verse. "God created man in His own image."

Sean looked up and caught his reflection in the dark window. Man—created to be perfect and in the image of God. Falling into death. And then came Jesus. The God-Man who gave his life so that God could create a New Man.

Sean fell down on his knees and dropped his head onto the soft leather of the Bible. He had no more arguments, no more debates. And no more reasons to resist.

"I'm guilty, Lord," he cried out. "But I accept Jesus as your Son and the payment for my sin. That he died when I should have

NEW CREATION

been the one dying and that He rose again so that I might live—truly, truly live as you created me to. And that I might be free."

Then, in that inexplicable moment, the hardened journalist broke down and sobbed. When he stopped crying, he stood, a new creation, put down the Bible and was about to walk to his room, ready to sleep peacefully for the first time in his life. It was the evening before the morning of the first day of the rest of his life.

A light in the window caught his attention just then and he moved toward it. He pushed back the curtain and gazed up. The rain had stopped, the clouds had parted, and there rising above the earth was... a glorious full moon.

CHAPTER SEVEN

Genesis 2:2 "And on the seventh day God ended His work which He had done, and He rested on the seventh day from all His work which He had done."

Sean sat in the courtroom as Gregory Van Heeder pleaded guilty to embezzlement and fraud. The judge, apparently happy about not having to go to trial, sentenced him to one year at the state penitentiary and several hours of community service after his release. Apparently Esmerelda's restitution had been a major factor in the judge's lenient sentence, since he mentioned it twice.

Esmerelda went up to hug her father as the policeman came to lead him out. Meanwhile, Sean slipped out the back and out to his car. When he reached his office, he slapped the draft of the last article on Gregory Van Heeder on Vance's desk.

NEW CREATION

"There you go, Ibsen. And I'm turning in my resignation."

"You're what?" Vance looked shocked, even as he handed the draft to another editor.

"I'm quitting. Taking a leave of absence. If you need two weeks notice, then I'm giving my two weeks notice and taking my two weeks of vacation until my last day."

"Sean, what are you talking about? This is a great job for you! They're maybe even talking Pulitzer Prize nomination. We've gotten so many comments on this story. Good ones. I think the publisher is very impressed!"

"Really, that's great," Sean answered, only a bit concerned.

"What's gotten into you, man?"

"That's what it is. I'm a new man, Vance, and I'm taking a leave of absence and going on Sabbatical for a year."

"Why?"

"Because that's how long Gregory Van Heeder is going to be in jail. If you want me to write a follow-up when he gets out, I will. I'm sure the Van Heeder family won't mind. Otherwise, I'm out that door."

Vance moved sluggishly as he followed Sean over to his desk. He still couldn't believe it.

"Sean, there were people from the *Tribune* calling for you!"

"Big deal."

"The *Tribune*!"

Sean ignored Vance's words.

CHAPTER SEVEN

Vance sighed as Sean started clearing out his desk. "I guess I can't stop you, Sean, but it's not a good job market out there."

"I know, Vance, but this is what God wants me to do."

"God? Do? Huh? What are you going to do?"

Sean looked off into the distance. "Rest. Rest in Him."

Vance watched as Sean started packing his things into a box and then turned and made his way back to his office, still trying to understand what had just happened.

But the newspaper business does not slow down for shocked editors and, within minutes, Vance had more things to take over his mind. At the end of the day, Sean stepped into his office.

"Well, I'm off now. See you later, Vance."

"Bye, Sean."

With a wave the men parted. Sean carried his box of possessions out to his car as Vance watched in confusion from the floor above.

CHAPTER EIGHT

Genesis 2:18, 22-23 "And the LORD God said, 'It is not good that man should be alone; I will make him a helper comparable to him.' Then the rib which the LORD God had taken from man He made into a woman, and He brought her to the man. And Adam said: 'This is now bone of my bones and flesh of my flesh; she shall be called Woman, because she was taken out of Man.'"

Sean watched the sun rise over the Wisconsin pine forest and sighed in happiness. He loved mornings. He looked down at the Bible in his lap and soaked in the verses for the day.

Over the last year, Sean had been living in an old hunting cabin of his grandfather's. Far from a busy lifestyle in Chicago, he'd had hours to spend reading the Bible and getting to know the God who had created the world and had made him a new man.

NEW CREATION

Sean the backwoodsman was almost a completely different person than Sean the city slicker. Sean wore flannel shirts and jeans every day, he'd grown a beard and mustache, and had even gotten used to some country music. He'd sold his crossover car for a "real man's vehicle"—a truck. It guzzled gas like nothing, but it was full of power and he loved it. He drove it to a library in a town several miles away to get Internet and check his e-mails; the only channels he got over his TV set showed either Packers or Brewers games, which was anathema to a true Chicagoan.

The fridge in the wooden cabin was small, and Sean had learned how to chop wood and start a fire early on in his time at the cabin. The highlights of his day were reading the Bible and perusing the few letters that came from his family or from Esmerelda, who wrote him every few weeks.

Of course there were the books, too. He piled up on books on creation, theology, history, government, politics. His entire mentality was being turned inside out and as he continued to read the Bible, more and more things Esmerelda had told him made sense. He had left his old worldview behind in Chicago and was being brainwashed—this time in the right mentality. And he enjoyed the mind cleansing.

But his year was almost up and it was time to reenter society. Vance had promised Sean a freelance column on Gregory Van Heeder's release and Sean had to be there to write it. Then it was time to get a job again. He'd done some freelance work while at the cabin, but that hadn't been much to live off of. Thankfully, he'd made friends who were good at hunting and they'd brought

CHAPTER EIGHT

some meat around for him. And he wasn't completely broke, but he was looking forward to being productive.

He would miss the quiet times with the Lord, though.

He stood and brushed the pine needles off his pants and headed toward his cabin.

Esmerelda stood with her aunt and uncle as they waited for Gregory to be released. She was excited for more than just getting to see her dad again. During his year in prison, he'd been broken enough to realize where true freedom lay—in the Lord. Her aunt and uncle had both gotten saved as well and were actively involved in their church's Bible studies.

Esmerelda rented a small apartment in one of the western suburbs and worked at a Christian school. Things had been hard for her in the last year, but it didn't matter. She was getting to see her father again.

"When will they let him out?" Esmerelda asked her uncle after waiting for several minutes.

Jarrod chuckled. "They have to process his papers."

"Oh."

She was so antsy she started pacing. She was thankful that the press wasn't out for this. With the governor's arrest several months ago, Gregory's story had become small news. The sound of a metal gate being opened alerted her and she spun around to see her father.

NEW CREATION

Gregory was wearing the suit he'd gone into jail wearing. He looked thinner, older, but the smile on his face was genuine.

"Essie," he called and she ran into his arms.

She burst into tears as he wrapped his arms around her. Gregory rubbed her back and placed numerous kisses on her forehead. He'd missed his daughter.

After hugging Essie, Gregory lightly embraced his sister and shook his brother-in-law's hand. Then he hugged Essie again.

From inside his car, parked some yards away from the family, Sean watched the reunion, a smile on his face.

At her apartment, Essie pulled out the sofa bed in her living room.

"I'm sorry I couldn't find a two-bedroom place," she told her dad as she threw the sofa pillows to the side.

"Oh, Hon. I'm just sorry that you are stuck living in this place after that beautiful house."

"It's okay, Dad."

"I really ruined your life, didn't I?"

"You made a mistake, but I forgive you. I'm just thankful that you didn't have to spend longer than a year in prison."

"Me, too. But what am I going to do for a job?"

Essie stood. "Have you ever considered being a teacher, Dad? You're one of the most mathematically and economically brilliant men I know. Surely you could find a place to teach."

CHAPTER EIGHT

Gregory's eyes drifted off. "Hmm, that might be interesting. I highly doubt I'll be vice president of a bank again."

"Doubtful. But we'll see what God provides."

Sean looked around his new office as the features editor for *Christian Perspective* magazine at Morning Star Communications. A leader in Christian media, Morning Star had jumped at the chance to have Sean on their staff, despite his year's Sabbatical from employment. They had been impressed by his final column for the *Daily Gazette* on Van Heeder's release and also some of the articles he'd done for *Field and Stream* and *Outdoor Life* while he had lived in Wisconsin.

He was looking forward to serving God and doing what he loved at Morning Star. Maybe he wouldn't win a Pulitzer Prize or edit the *USA Today* or *New York Times*, but you could not have found a more content man in Chicagoland at that moment.

Almost.

After setting up the items on his desk, Sean realized it was missing a very important item. A family picture.

Esmerelda was so pleased for her Dad. It really was a miraculous answer to prayer. A mid-sized college near her apartment had offered Gregory a job teaching macro and micro economics in the spring. The job came with a lot of strings attached, but he

NEW CREATION

was excited about teaching. Even though she was excited for him, her heart was heavy. In the last month, she hadn't received any letters from Sean.

The two had written to each other on a regular basis when he'd lived in Wisconsin. He never left a return address on his letters, so she had mailed them to his grandparents, and they had forwarded her letters to him. His letters had been so full of what he was learning from the Bible. In his first letter, he'd told her about his new life and she'd cried over it, wishing she'd known on the day of the pre-trial, but happy for him anyway. But after a year, his letters had stopped. She wondered where he was at that moment.

A month after her father's release, on a chilly October day, she received a call from *Christian Perspective* magazine about an interview concerning her and her father's testimonies. At first she wasn't sure if she should answer it, but in an impulsive move she agreed when the woman told her it was just a preliminary meeting.

"Great," the woman answered. "We'll have you meet with our features editor next Tuesday. Is that satisfactory?"

"Yes, it is."

"Fantastic. I'll pencil you in and we'll see you on Tuesday."

"All right."

On Tuesday, she dressed in khaki slacks and a blue corduroy jacket over a striped silk blouse. She pulled her hair back so that all the attention was drawn to her eyes. Stepping back and look-

CHAPTER EIGHT

ing in the mirror, she approved of her look. She grabbed her purse and headed out to the Morning Star building in a far western suburb.

When she arrived, she waited in the lobby for the editor to meet her. She was sitting on the couch lost in thought when she heard a familiar voice.

"Are you here to apply to be one of my reporters?"

She looked up in surprise and her eyes met Sean's twinkling brown ones.

"Sean!" she gasped as she stood excitedly.

He laughed as he came her way. She moved forward and then hesitated. He held out his arms and hugged her.

"Hello, Essie. How are you?"

"I'm good, how are you? What are you doing here?"

He stepped back and his mouth curled into a grin. "I'm the features editor here at Morning Star. It was my idea to interview you, so I had my secretary set up this meeting. But the real reason was to see you again. The letters were great, but it's nothing like getting to discuss things with you in person."

She blushed. "You mean argue, don't you?"

"I don't think we ever argued. Disagreed yes, argued no. Hope you don't mind going out to lunch before the interview, do you?"

She shook her head. "Nope."

"Good."

NEW CREATION

He signed out at the receptionist's desk and then headed out with his arm gently clasping Essie's elbow. They went to lunch at a nice restaurant and caught up with each other's lives. Essie felt a little odd as they ate.

"It feels a bit strange without you pressing me with questions," she admitted.

He grinned. "Do you want me to conduct the interview right now?"

She paused and then shook her head. "Nope. It's a horrible way to ruin a lovely lunch."

The smile never left his face. "Ah, Essie, always so proper."

A blush spread across her face. "You're teasing me, aren't you?"

He nodded. "Yep."

When they finished, Sean drove them to Morton Arboretum. The fall leaves were spectacular that time of year and the Arboretum was the best place to see them.

"I cleared all afternoon of appointments so that I could spend this time with you," he admitted as he helped her from the car.

"Are we even going to do an interview?" she asked knowingly.

"Of course. But not now."

They walked along the path, enjoying the nice day and the vivid colors of the leaves.

"So, you're features editor?"

"Yep. I love it. And you?"

CHAPTER EIGHT

"Nothing special, administrative assistant at a school. They don't let me help in the business office, though," she said with a grin.

He laughed out loud as she joined in. When their laughs had subsided, he reached down and grabbed her hand.

"Essie."

"Yes, Sean?"

He stopped and looked into her eyes. "You opened my eyes up to many things, Esmerelda. Without you, I would probably still be blinded to spiritual things, thinking only of being editor of the *New York Times* or something."

"I don't deserve your gratefulness, Sean," she responded humbly.

"Too bad, I'm giving it to you anyway."

"What were you going to say?"

He lifted her hand and laced his fingers through hers.

"Do you remember what God did after He created man?"

She nodded. "Yes, He paraded the animals in front of Adam so that Adam could name them."

"Exactly. And among them there was found no companion for Adam. That was my life last year, Essie. I was surrounded by animals that I thought only belonged in zoos or wildlife reserves. And although I was alone with God, which was wonderful, I hoped that He would look down and say about me what He did about Adam: 'It's not good that he is alone.' And He did. When

NEW CREATION

I look at you, I know that you are the helper that God created for me."

Tears sprung in Essie's eyes as Sean picked up her left hand in between his own hands.

"You're my rib, Essie, without you, I'm incomplete." He dropped to one knee and pulled out a ring. "Will you marry me, Essie?"

The tears turned to laughter and she smiled brightly. "Yes, yes. I'll marry you, Sean!"

He stood and wrapped her in an embrace as the wind showered them in golden and crimson leaves.

Breinigsville, PA USA
28 September 2010
246295BV00003B/49/P